Click, Clack, Surprise!

Click, Clack, SURPRISE!

Doreen Cronin
illustrated by Betsy Lewin

A Caitlyn Dlouhy Book

ATHENEUM BOOKS FOR YOUNG READERS
New York   London   Toronto   Sydney   New Delhi

atheneum

Click, Clack, Surprise!

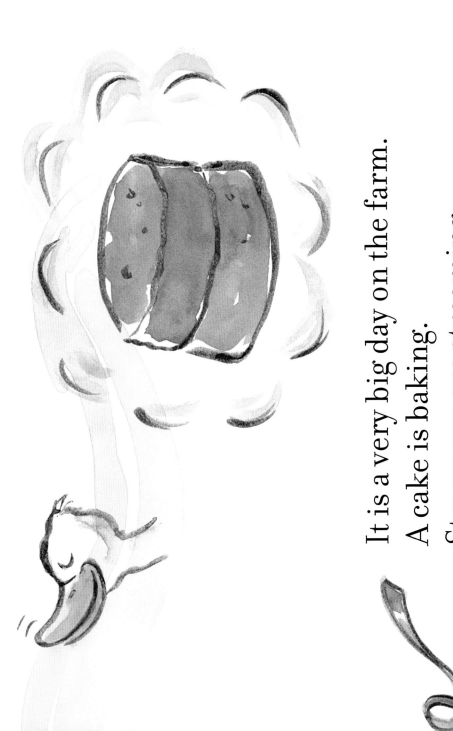

It is a very big day on the farm.
A cake is baking.
Streamers are streaming.
Mice are floating past the window.

The invitations have been delivered.

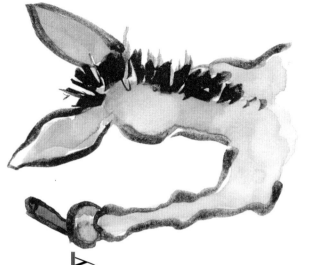

Pin the Tail on the Donkey **Canceled** by Donkey.

Duck, Duck, Goose **Canceled** by Goose.

Steal the Bacon **Canceled** by Anonymous Request.

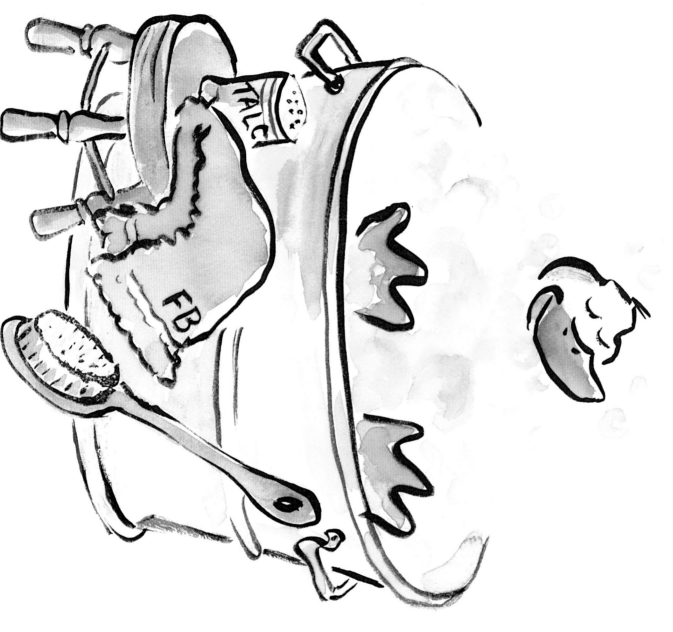

Everybody wants to look their best
for Little Duck's party.

Duck takes a long, hot bubble bath to look
his best.

He
rub‑a‑dubs,

rub‑a‑dubs,

rub‑a‑dubs clean.

And walks on over to the maple tree.

Little Duck watches and then rub-a-dubs too.

The sheep need a trim to look their best.

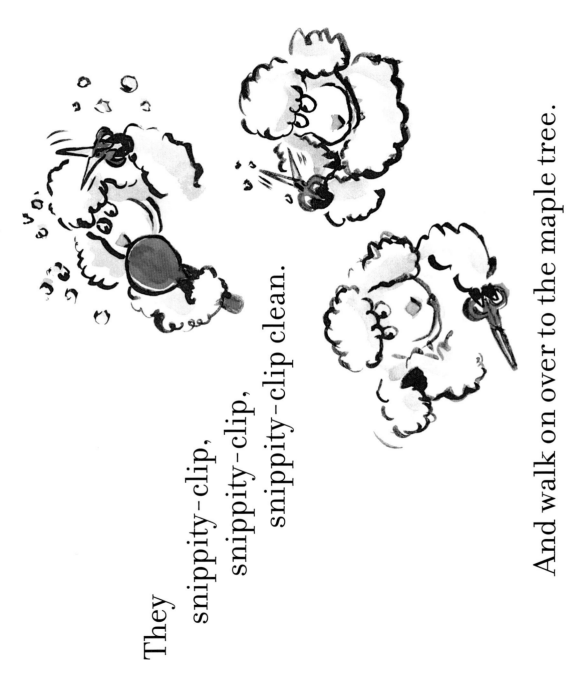

They
snippity-clip,
snippity-clip,
snippity-clip clean.

And walk on over to the maple tree.

Little Duck watches
and then snippity-clips too.

The cat wants to look her best.

She
slurp-a-lurps,

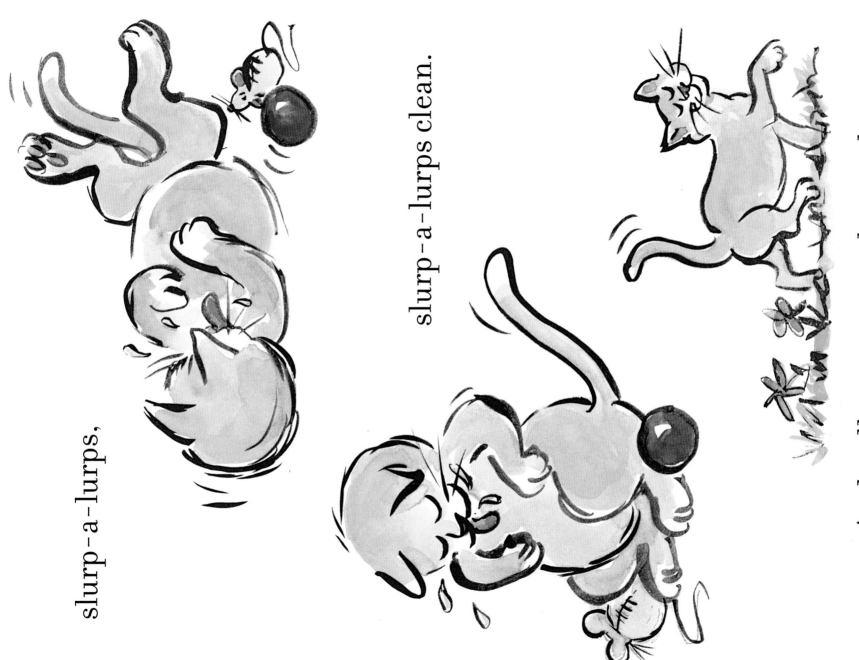

slurp-a-lurps,

slurp-a-lurps clean.

And walks on over to the maple tree.

Little Duck
watches and then
slurp-a-lurps too.

The chickens take a dust bath to look their best.

They shimmy-shake,

shimmy-shake,

shimmy-shake clean.

And walk on over to the maple tree.

Little Duck watches
and then shimmy-shakes too.

The pigs need a mud bath to feel their best.

They
squish and squash,

squish and squash,
squish and squash clean.

And walk on over to the maple tree.

Little Duck watches
and then squishes
and squashes too.

The cows like themselves just the way they are.

No rub-a-dubbing.
No snippity-clipping.
No slurp-a-lurping.
No shimmy-shaking.
No squish and squashing.

They walk on over to the maple tree.

Farmer Brown frosts the cake,

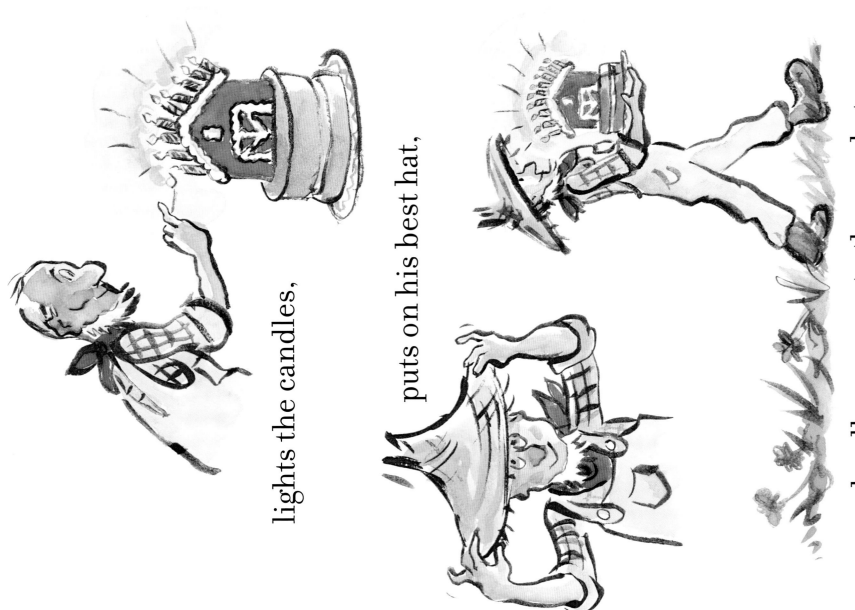

lights the candles,

puts on his best hat,

and walks on over to the maple tree.

Happy Birthday to you,

Happy Birthday to . . .

ewww!

A birthday surprise for *everyone,* under the maple tree.

For Ryleigh Elizabeth
—D. C.

For Ted, who has had eighty surprises so far
—B. L.

atheneum

ATHENEUM BOOKS FOR YOUNG READERS
An imprint of Simon & Schuster Children's Publishing Division
1230 Avenue of the Americas, New York, New York 10020
Text copyright © 2016 by Doreen Cronin
Illustrations copyright © 2016 by Betsy Lewin

ATHENEUM BOOKS FOR YOUNG READERS is a registered trademark of Simon & Schuster, Inc.
Atheneum logo is a trademark of Simon & Schuster, Inc.
For information about special discounts for bulk purchases, please contact Simon & Schuster Special
Sales at 1-866-506-1949 or business@simonandschuster.com.
The Simon & Schuster Speakers Bureau can bring authors to your live event. For more information
or to book an event, contact the Simon & Schuster Speakers Bureau at 1-866-248-3049 or visit our
website at www.simonspeakers.com.
Book design by Ann Bobco
The text for this book was set in Filosofia.
The illustrations for this book were rendered in pen, ink, and watercolor.
Manufactured in China
0616 SCP
First Edition
10 9 8 7 6 5 4 3 2 1
CIP data for this book is available from the Library of Congress.
ISBN 978-1-4814-7031-5
ISBN 978-1-4814-7032-2 (eBook)